Stinky Owl

Melanie Burgess

Headline Kids
an imprint of **Headline Books, Inc.**
Terra Alta, WV

Stinky Owl

by Melanie Burgess

To order additional copies of this book, or for book publishing information, or to contact the author:

Headline Kids
P. O. Box 52
Terra Alta, WV 26764

Email: mybook@headlinebooks.com
www.headlinebooks.com

Ashley Teets—*Art Director*
Lucas Kelly—*Design/Layout*

Published by Headline Books
Headline Kids is an imprint of Headline Books

ISBN-13: 9781946664303

Library of Congress Control Number: 2018938073

PRINTED IN THE UNITED STATES OF AMERICA

I would like to dedicate this book to my family. To my husband David, you are my beloved lowercase king. To my daughter Megan Ellifritz you are my pearl of great price. To my daughter Grace Burgess you are my blessing of God. To my son Matthew Ellifritz you are my gift of God. I love you all more than you can imagine!

Acknowledgments

Andrew Wommack founder of Andrew Wommack Ministries and Charis Bible College for his Sowers Seminar and his teaching, "What's in your hand." It was through listening to these teachings that faith arose in me to believe God for a creative idea.

Megan Manes a naturalist at Rocky Gap State park. It was during her teaching at a program "Hungry, hungry, hoot owls," that the idea for this story was birthed.

Sarah Milbourne Rocky Gap State Park manager for helping me to get all the facts correct about each bird of prey and for giving me her full support on this project.

Thanks

I would like to thank God for giving me the ability to draw. Jesus for taking my sins in his own body, providing salvation for me and bringing me into a right relationship with God. And the Holy Spirit that gave me all the ideas for this book along with the words to the story. I love you so much!

There once lived a Great Horned Owl.
He had no friends because he smelled fowl.

He stunk really bad you see,
for he had no sense of smell
like you and me, and because
of that his most favorite snack
was a stinky old skunk, and
that's a fact.

He enjoyed many other meals: mice, frogs, rabbits, and moles. They all left his taste buds full of holes.

Skunk is what he craved, it was his most favorite treat, and it made his diet utterly complete.

One day,
flying by his
nest was the
Barred Owl
on his own hunting
quest. The Great Horn's
plumicorns stood straight
up with glee. Could
someone really be coming
to see me?

His joy quickly went away when Barred Owl didn't want to stay.

He just made jokes as he went on his way. "Who cooks for you, who cooks for you? Someone who makes stinky stew?"

Later that night, Great Horn had quite the fright. A little further down the way lived two sister Barn Owls who wanted to play.

Great Horn was
finishing his meal that
was rank, and most
definitely stank, while
the sisters were busy
planning a prank.

They used a skunk tail attached to some yarn to lure him right into their barn.

Then with a sheet clinched tightly in their feet, they flew down from their post. Great Horn shrieked, "Oh no! It must be a ghost!"

Great Horn realized that he had been fooled. He really didn't like being ridiculed.

The sisters taunted as he began to walk away slow, "You smell so bad, don't you know? Why don't you just go?" Great Horn hung his head down low and went away in deep sorrow.

"Nobody likes me," Great Horn said to himself with a groan. "I just need one friend so I'm not so alone."

The very next day, after having some skunk, he saw two Screech Owls by the old tree trunk. Little did he know how badly he stunk.

15

"Maybe I can go say hello. Maybe they will like me, you never know."

The Screech Owls could smell Great Horn's stink in the air. "Let's fly away," one said.

"We can't," said the other. "He is right over there!"

"What will we do? We need a disguise, one that will fool Great Horns very keen eyes."

They used their own camouflage
against the old Indian Trail Marker tree.

Great Horn thought, "Was that a mirage? Were there Screech Owls I did see?"

Later that day, feeling quite grim, he saw two Bald Eagles going for a swim. He spoke to them from out on a limb. "Hello, my friends! It's a beautiful day!"

"It was until we got a whiff of you," they said. "Please go away!"

20

Great Horn once again felt really sad,
wishing for one friend that he had.

From out of nowhere, Great Horn's arch enemy appeared! "Stinky owl! Stinky owl!" they laughed and cheered.

"Those two Red-tailed Hawks are as mean as they could be, they are always picking on me!"

Looking up to the sky, Great Horn saw the Hybrid Falcon soaring by. "He flies so fast. Speeds up to 200 miles per hour. Why, I'm sure, even he thinks I smell sour!"

Little did he know things were about to turn around. Two Black Vultures, who lived in the campground, saw Great Horn's solemn despair. They wanted to help. They really did care.

"Great Horn is actually a really nice owl. I don't know why everyone thinks he smells fowl. His smell doesn't bother us. It doesn't make us ill. As a matter of fact, it's no worse than roadkill."

"I've got it!" one vulture cried. "I know what to do. Let's introduce him to the female Great Horn." And away they flew.

The vultures' plan was a hit. The two owls liked each other quite a bit.

The next few weeks were the best they had ever been. Great Horn saw the female again and again and again.

They laughed, they played, they hunted, they flew.

The best part is, they even enjoyed a skunk or two.
  The female shared in Great Horn's need for such a catch. She absolutely loved skunk, making them the perfect match!

Great Horn asked her to be his wife, and now they each have a friend for life.

Never again was Great Horn sad, lonely, or depressed, and they always had plenty of skunk in their nest.

How wonderful it is to be so blessed.

Did you know?

Indian Trail Marker Tree
A tree bent as a sapling by Native American Indians to mark their trails.

The Great Horned Owl
"The tiger of the night sky" because of their keen eyesight and expert hunting skills. Although it is portrayed in this story that the birds could smell Stinky Owl, most birds of prey, particularly with the Great Horned Owl, do not have a sense of smell. The author disregarded that fact for the purpose of storytelling.

The Barred Owl
A distinct whoo-hoo-hoo-hoo whoo-hoo-hoo-hoo-oo call which sounds like, "who cooks for you, who cooks for you all?"

The Barn Owl
Sometimes referred to as ghost owls.

Eastern Screech Owl
One of the smallest of the owl species.

The Bald Eagle
Bald Eagles have see-through eyelids, called a nictitating membrane.

Red-Tailed Hawks
Frequently referred to as a "chicken hawk."

The Black Vulture
Vultures serve an important purpose of cleaning the environment and limiting the spread of disease.